T0090493

BREXITEER

BY
THE LUCKY MAN

authorHOUSE®

AuthorHouse™ UK
1663 Liberty Drive
Bloomington, IN 47403 USA
www.authorhouse.co.uk
Phone: UK TFN: 0800 0148641 (Toll Free inside the UK)
UK Local: (02) 0369 56322 (+44 20 3695 6322 from outside the UK)

Published by AuthorHouse 09/14/2023

ISBN: 979-8-8230-8473-4 (sc)
ISBN: 979-8-8230-8474-1 (e)

Library of Congress Control Number: 2023917493

Print information available on the last page.

Contents

1

Voluntary Mission

English-speaking people started receiving intel on a secret plan to make the remaining European Union fit to join the British Commonwealth of Nations. No facial recognition was allowed to help prevent any part of an operation becoming compromised.

This in 2022, a year that saw the death of the longest-serving monarch in the history of the United Kingdom, Queen Elizabeth II, a reign that outlasted the membership of the UK in the politics of Eurolanda.

This year, on Saturday, 6 May 2023, the coronation of King Charles III took place. May the refashioned European Union become a real gift to him and his reign from grateful English-speaking people worldwide.

2

International Leggings Brigade

The International Leggings Brigade was formed from volunteers (from all walks of life!) continuing in their daytime activities while awaiting nighttime operations in Eurolanda. There they identify Europhiliacs and other undesirables for capture by the Pixie Hat Brigade. They are transferred by a Merlin HM Mk2 helicopter to an awaiting container ship.

Once full, the giant vessel heads for a former penal colony down under. Here, the long march begins to the centre of the continent. The purpose is to construct the largest man-made sea and inland resort in the world—a task that could last a lifetime, reduce above-average population density in Europe, and be of major benefit to climatic considerations of the present political debate. Again, the struggle for completion will be a victory for English-speaking people and unknown warriors!

Rumours that 007 was in town were quelled today despite the appearance of an Aston Martin just off High Street.

Talk has it that he will mastermind the search for the source of an invasive species taking over hilltops that is capable of wading through seas. The three-bladed wind turbine injures and kills sea and migrating wild birds wherever they go, a practice outlawed in the United Kingdom during the reign of Queen Elizabeth II. So far the speculative climate change argument has got the better of politicians throughout Eurolanda.

Save our wild birds. Save our feathered friends. Rage against the wind machines!

3

All Blacks

Just returned from a night raid into Eurolanda, our unidentified volunteer stops by for a beverage. Updated with the latest intel, which could see our recruit return by the Merlin helicopter into the drop zone. Wine bars are known to be frequented by Euromaniacs, with their careless talk of business supremacy infiltrating the night air. For them, a lifetime of toil with hand tools and the international minimum wage could be the next step on the career ladder, accumulated for them either in euros or British pounds, as is their choice. Will they back the winners?

4

Dazzling Camouflage

Camouflage was designed to give our volunteers of the International Leggings Brigade the advantage over climate speculators and their careless talk in wine bars throughout Eurolanda. Their temporary fixation on the patterns can lure them into a false sense of awareness. The Pixie Hat Brigade waiting nearby bundle them into a crate, and they are soon on their way to our container ship. Emptied into the confines of such, they eventually awake with hangovers to be fed on past sell-by-date supermarket sandwiches, traditional recipe gruel, and a saltwater drink. Groans are ignored as the vessel sets the GPS for a former penal colony down under. Costs of the half world cruise are deducted from their international minimum wage remuneration once hard labour begins.

5

8 June 1946

Today We Celebrate Victory

> I send this personal message to you and all other boys and girls at school. For you have shared in the hardships and dangers of total war and you have shared in the triumphs no less of the Allied Nations.
>
> I know you will always feel proud to belong to a country which was capable of such supreme effort; proud, too, of parents and elder brothers and sisters who, by their courage, endurance, and enterprise brought victory. May these qualities be yours as you grow up and join in the common effort to establish among the nations of the world unity and peace.

The above is a copy of a message sent to schoolchildren from His Majesty, King George V. The United Nations organisation began the previous year in 1945.

6

Alnoth the Staller

My earliest recorded ancestor was an English thegn[1] in the army of King Harold, who fought the Normans in the famous Battle of Hastings in 1066. Remarkably, he went on to serve King William the Conqueror as master of the house, a position still of the royal household to this day. He was granted several manors and a castle in Lincolnshire, leading historians to believe he had married into royalty to have received such wealth. A few single Danish princesses were about at the time, and some historical records named one as Lividia. The pair settled into a manor at Meriet in Somerset and had a son named Hardinge.

The defeated sons of King Harold fled to Ireland and there raised an army to challenge the Norman conquest. They landed by ship on the coast of Somerset. They were met by Alnoth (Ælfnoth) and his forces, and battle took place somewhere near the hill Brent Knoll. Despite victory, Alnoth was slain.

King William took pity on the orphan Hardinge and paid for him to have an education in Bristol.

[1] A thegn carried out local duties, such as guarding tax collectors from attack and organising the repair of fortifications, roads, and bridges.

7

Troupe Train

Our specially charted rail transport takes volunteers to the seaside resorts of southern England. Here they will learn beach skills, including covert sunbathing. Evenings see initiative training in nearby wine bars and beer taverns, simulating those of Eurolanda.

Admiral Haddock is overall commander in chief who has ordered our container ship to anchor in the Bristol Channel. The city played a major part in the historic Atlantic slave trade, and before that, trading slaves into Ireland. Poorer families could sell off their surplus kids and make a tidy sum for retirement.

The Merlin helicopter and its chums play their part in rehearsals, hoisting empty containers between Eurolanda and our container ship.

Undesirables will eventually enjoy a half world cruise to a former penal colony down under.

8

God's Wonderful Railways

Steam locomotives were the invention of Great Britain. Various railway companies provided a network of routes spanning out from the capital, London. It was the Great Western Railway Company (GWR) that received the accolade God's Wonderful Railway. It was chief engineer Isambard Kingdom Brunel (IKB) who not only designed the routes following the contours of the west country but also the station buildings. Passengers could get a ticket to New York by train first and then by his ship, the SS *Great Britain*, now preserved in her original dry dock at Bristol Harbour. To get to the open sea, she had to pass under Clifton Suspension Bridge—the first of its type designed by IKB and still in use today. His Bristol Temple Meads railway station still serves the city, and the GWR logo can be seen in the original seats.

9

Hampton Grandad MM

At the beginning of the First World War in 1914, mounted regiments of the British army were sent to France as part of an expeditionary force. In order to maintain sufficient numbers in the United Kingdom, a recruitment campaign began for reservists.

My grandfather Taylor volunteered after a few years in the Merchant Navy, having left school.

The Royal Buckingham Hussars took him on, and he was based in Windsor Great Park below the castle. Four horses pulled a lumber and gun carriage with him as a rider. His army title was then Driver 3319 Albert Edward Taylor. This was awarded to soldiers who completed a medic's course with the Royal Army Medical Corps.

Later, mounted regiments were largely disbanded when it became clear that horse-drawn transports were no longer suitable for modern warfare. He was transferred for training to become an infantryman and sharpshooter in 1916 at the age of twenty-two. MM stands for military medal, which was awarded to him for gallantry in the field in 1918.

Hampton Grandad was a family name to distinguish him from Standish Grandad, my maternal grandfather.

10

Enduring Freedom

The muffled groans of captives can just be heard outside this shipping container. Climate activists and other undesirables make for the bulk of the cargo.

The Merlin helicopter will be along soon to hoist the crated captives to our vessel anchored in the Bristol Channel. Stacked neatly one on top of the other, the load will soon be underway out on to the Severn Sea.

Admiral Haddock at the wheel will navigate through the Mediterranean Sea and Suez Canal and continue to a former penal colony down under. The centre of the continent was chosen for the largest man-made lake in the world, more like an inland sea. Connected to the Pacific Ocean by a navigable canal, it will feed the artificial lake. Fish and other edible seafood are soon arriving to take advantage of the new habitat.

Captives working in the heat of the desert will have contributed something of enduring value to the natural resources of the world. Those who try to make a run from their toil will face tormenting creatures at home in the inhospitable surroundings, including scorpions, for one, with their deadly stinging tails by day and black mamba poisonous snakes at night. Freshwater, a major lacking, will be a major threat to their own mortal existence.

However, over the decades and centuries to come, a new inland resort will take shape for the benefit of all humankind. Survivors from the original task force will have unique stories to tell when they next visit a wine bar or beer tavern!

11

International Leggings Brigade

One of our troopers just returned from a lying-up position in the Arctic, wrapping his hands around a hot beverage before being thoroughly debriefed.

The two main requirements for joining our elite team in the snow: being able bodied and capable.

Europhiles may choose the snowy waste route as a way out of Eurolanda. Capture would mean a lifetime of toil for them in the middle of the Outback down under. Recycled food products provide their staple diet, and sterilised, bottled waste liquids quench their thirst.

With the whole area surrounded by aboriginals on a war footing, the chances of escape are zero!

12

New Appointment

Admiral Haddock kindly gave up his time to steer our container ship down under. He will now return to his more usual duties in a fishery protection role.

His replacement, Admiral Codpiece, has vast experience in the naval area and should keep our volunteer crews on their toes if not their backs.

13

Wind Turbines

These have always had a suspicious look about them. Displaying monstrous-sized towers featuring the three-bladed logo of a central European motor industry is a case in point. Who is the berc in a merc anyway?

Ludicrously aired as an answer to global warming, the clueless eco-scientists failed to calculate the long-term effects of continuously taking power from the wind. As any fool knows, it would reduce the cooling effect of wind on the earth's surface, thereby adding to global warming.

Hundreds if not thousands of wild or migrating birds flying at low altitudes have been injured or even killed by their moving blades, thus adding the interests of conservation as another reason for not having the monotonous monsters at all.

Fortunately, wind turbine demolition companies have now come into being and hopefully will become a growth business to combat the menace of this twenty-first-century madness.

Resembling a First World War machine gun post (pill box), our observers watch the town centre for any insurgent activity. Cunningly disguised as a mailbox, passers-by rarely give it a glance. It even has the cipher of King George V (GR) to give it further credibility.

Our lookouts search for anyone suspiciously acting like a Europhile, a climate protestor, or a leaflet distributor. The latter may have already ensured that more trees have been cut down to produce the printed matter and are lobbying for more trees to be planted!

Joined up finking baffles the man in the street who is readily approached and offered the offending material. As for the few remaining Europhiles who now resemble a dirty raincoat ensemble, the arguments for rejoining the Euromaniacs are thin. Few if any have bothered to cycle in because of the inclement weather and stand there blaming Brexit for climate change!

They have a look of solidarity with the climate protestors who claim that the weather was different 250,000 years ago, and unless it changes again in the next 250,000, we are all doomed to be wiped out by a meteorite. The madness of our times: Brexiteer!

14

When the Bluebirds are Over

Only a provincial town in the West Country said to be the best inland resort in the country whose broad Promenade was described as the finest street in England, when opened, could feature a feral pigeon as its heraldic beast! It is featured on the town crest, on top of signposts, and here depicted nesting.

When a good doctor passed through the small country town centuries ago, he spotted a pigeon drinking from a spa water spring. He took a sample to London and discovered it was health giving. The discovery began the transformation of the town into a spa resort, much of which we see today.

However, the heroic bird was more likely to have been a wood pigeon, the most numerous of any bird type throughout the land as the area was more wooded and rural back then.

Flocks of feral pigeons are attracted to built-up areas and cities where they spend much of their time courting and a cooing and getting under your feet whilst feeding on breadcrumbs and fast food debris.

Anyway, good luck to our feathered friends!

15

Charles Thomas Browning

My great-grandfather Browning was employed by the Stroud Brewing Company, Salmon Springs, near Pitchcombe, Gloucestershire, before enlisting in the British army. The coming Boer War saw men volunteer at the turn of last century. He joined the Gloucestershire Regiment as a foot soldier who, by then, were wearing the legendary back badge on their helmets. My maternal grandmother, Florence Mary Browning, recalled that she saw him for the only time wearing his uniform. Her mother had already died in childbirth.

After the wars, a ship carrying our troops home experienced an outbreak of scarlet fever, and he unfortunately died. My grandmother was raised as an orphan by a family who knew her father.

The British army by then had switched to khaki uniforms. The 303 Lee-Enfield rifle had become the first standard-issue type to be used by the troops. A trained rifleman could fire off fifteen rounds a minute when required with good range and accuracy. It was used throughout the First and Second World Wars as well as for ceremonial duties to be replaced in the 1950s by the SLR (self-loading rifle).

As a teenage member of the Air Training Corps during the 1970s, I was allowed to fire the 303 at an outdoor range near Awre in Gloucestershire. They said beware of the kick (recoil). It kicked!

16

Pixie Hat Regiment

A Special Aid Service (SAS) formed to provide support on the ground for our International Leggings Brigade.

Veteran volunteers are grateful to get away from the boredom of daytime television. Staying up to see anything worthwhile after the 9pm watershed can find the senile viewer asleep on the sofa with the TV still blaring away, no doubt included as a viewer by the broadcasting companies in the national viewing statistics and used as a lobby for more government funds for minority interests.

Now that TV is a minority interest in itself, thanks to laptop and smartphone social media usage, only the multitaskers can watch a soap and text aunty Mary at the same time. Now that white male gender types have been largely made redundant from national debate, their new usage in the affairs of the country has been a welcome asset to our Pixie Hat Regiment.

Uniforms are provided quite inexpensively from any of the numerous charity shops that now adorn our traditional shopping centres. Experience from the University of Life is a course they have all completed prior to receiving the state pension award.

Legal tender in the form of coin of the realm still accompanies their financial transactions. The new yeomanry of the United Kingdom are now armed with a bus pass in their holsters and a free newspaper to break the monotony of transit to and from the suburbs.

17

Good Friday Eve 2023

In many respects, it's been one of those days. The main mission is to collect my late mother's ashes from the funeral directors and take them to her former retirement flat near Gloucester.

And there they were, sitting on a shelf in a colourful cardboard cylinder inside a rather fancy-looking tall shopping bag tied up with string.

It looked like I might have bought something from an expensive retail outlet when taking them onto the bus for the journey from Hucclecote to Wotton Pitch all along Ermine Street, a former Roman road.

They were placed unceremoniously on a chair next to the French windows at her former flat and left there in state for their final journey tomorrow morning.

Many years ago, about 2014, she had said to me she would like her ashes scattered on Haresfield Beacon. The Cotswold Hills outlier was an ancient British hillfort in the era before Roman conquest. Inhabitants would have had fantastic distant views of the River

Severn estuary to the south west and the now Royal Forest of Dean to the west.

Anyhow, it was her favourite hill as a child overlooking Standish below, where she lived, and the hamlet of Arlebrook, where she had friends and relatives. So the final journey for her ashes is on Good Friday tomorrow. As her next of kin, fulfilling her final wishes seems like the least I can do.

18

Coining It

Despite a growing tendency to a use a debit or credit card for small-value transactions, legal tender has some interesting features. The coin of the realm frequently includes commemorative designs on the reverse of £2 and 50p pieces.

The four hundredth anniversary of playwright William Shakespeare was commemorated with three different £2 coins in 2016. The one in my collection is for the play *Macbeth,* one of his most famous.

Commemorative coins often appear randomly in change and make for a nice way to accumulate some savings, all of them worth more than face value to collectors.

The inscription around the edge of the coin reads The Hollow Crown, and the obverse has a portrait of Queen Elizabeth II D G REG F D: *Dei Gratia Regina Fidei Defensor:* By Grace of God Monarch Defender of the Faith. Rather apt for any Easter weekend celebrations.

19

10 Bob Note

Prior to decimalisation we had a ten shilling: the 10 bob note. Prior to decimalisation, we had a ten shilling banknote in circulation. Two were worth a UK pound. Shillings were a coin worth 5p in today's money, but ten of them were worth the same as the colloquial ten bob note.

After decimalisation, a seven-sided coin known as the 50 pence piece was introduced but was equivalent to ten shillings. After resizing downwards, some of them started to feature commemorative designs like the £2 coins.

In late 2022, one appeared in my change featuring Charles III, not due to have been released until 2023. Even more puzzling is that the king was yet to have a coronation, not taking place until Saturday, 6 May 2023. If he were to abdicate prior, I might have a rare coin in my possession.

20

Thoughts of England

Having been born here, there is no doubt that it is steeped in history. The language itself started appearing in written form during the Anglo-Saxon era. However, its roots go back much further.

Mother and Father may have central European or Latin origins and is used in the official language of the nation. However, *Ma and Pa* may be heard speaking from the French-influenced *Mama and Papa*. More than likely, an overseas student of the English language heard *Mum and Dad* spoken especially in conversations involving family.

Both my parents used Mum and Dad when talking about my grandparents, but from when or where did these two descriptive words originate?

Simplistically, research suggests that the language of the ancient British featured one-syllable words. Mum and Dad fit that category. Modern dictionaries may describe them as being of common or vulgar usage. So that's how the literary educated types regard us, common and vulgar! The person in the streets of English towns and cities may well use the common vernacular but break into a politer version when dealing with authorities and the like.

So to get by in our own country, we need to know at least two versions. One we learnt in the playgrounds and the other in the classrooms! Regional dialects add to the mix, and I doubt if there is anyone in the country or abroad that uses exactly the same English vocabulary, making us all unique as the English-speaking people we are!

21

Teatime

When the Tudor Dynasty finally freed us from the yoke of the Holy Roman Empire, the nation was freer to determine its own future. Whilst the unknowing in Europe were still preaching that the world was flat, the British got on and expanded its merchant navy fleet. A Royal exchange was opened in London and acted as an early stock market, allowing the financing of the new merchant adventurers to develop a fleet like the world had never seen before. As well, London, Bristol, and Liverpool expanded as ports and busied themselves importing and exporting with all parts of the globe.

Somehow in the depths of China it discovered tea, a beverage we have long since been famous for. With approval at the highest level, tea inspired a whole new growth industry. It came off the ships in tea chests with a long, long shelf and storage life.

Tea shops were opened, and with the different varieties of the dried leaves came morning tea, afternoon tea and evening tea. To drink it we had to have teacups and saucers. Staffordshire found itself overwhelmed by demand for its China clay resources to make the items needed, including teapots and tea plates. The area became known as the Potteries as a result. Silver was used to make teaspoons, tea strainers, and silver-plated items, further reducing costs and adding to the demand for Sheffield steel made in Yorkshire. After tea came the washing up, and Ireland contributed the linen for tea cloths.

Teatime was another excuse for a family to get together whilst those earning a living got a tea break. It transformed the growing civil service, who were offered tea at their offices, reducing trips to local pubs at lunchtimes for alcoholic beverages.

Before long, a whole new class of people emerged and were to stay: the middle classes. In Europe were the extremes—extremely rich or extremely poor—with the vast majority falling into the latter category. In Britain, over time, the middle classes grew in number and became the most influential in the country. Starvation as a cause of death was eventually largely wiped out and health remarkably improved by the introduction of the welfare state. Drawbacks that affected Britain's wealth creating society was largely warfare. European countries conspired together to halt England in her tracks, but an expansion of her royal navy rather than her land armies saw that the continental state-sponsored detractors were overwhelmed by the formidable seamanship of this maritime nation.

22

Admiral Kirk

Famed for his handling of the USS *Enterprise,* he has agreed to take temporary command of our growing Eurolanda fleet. Here we see him crossing the Atlantic in a barque from a previous era. As for him, time travel is no problem.

The growing concern is economic migrants trying to enter as illegal immigrants. As the cost of housing or hoteling them rises, alternatives are being sought. One measure is to transport them to the centre of a former penal colony down under and build the largest man-made sea in the world.

International minimum wage standards apply and payments of their choice are in either euros or UK pounds, depending whether they consider themselves winners or losers. After deductions for accommodation and sustenance, income tax, and national insurance, the remainder is invested for their dotage. A remarkable coup for the UK treasury and a remarkable inland resort for the benefit of humanity!

23

Admiral Kirk, Part II

Our guest commander has crossed the Atlantic Ocean to be with our volunteer Eurolanda fleet, remaining onboard his own starship for the duration of his commanding influence. Crews keep watch for Europhiles trying to escape by sea. Many are burdened by the weight of euros they attempt to carry. The near-worthless currency carried in sacks weighs down their chosen vessels, and our voluntary tall ships are able to track them down.

The 'tracking device' is known as Spock.

Distributed to the fleet captains bringing them into the future age of cyber technology, the unfortunates are hauled aboard and given a traditional bygone welcome involving the lash. Stored in the holds below, they are fed on discarded supermarket meal-deal sandwiches, Olde English recipe cold gruel, and a saltwater drink.

When the holds are full, the Spock navigates them to our nearest container ship for the journey to a former penal colony down under. The half world cruise includes container cabins and a chance to socialise with fellow miscreants. The central desert awaits and a bucket and spade each to begin the digging of a handmade inland sea. The task is lifelong in near unbearable conditions but is a major future benefit for all humanity.

24

Last Stand of the 2nd Devons

On 26 May 1918, the 2nd Battalion, Devonshire Regiment was sent up to defend a position known as the Bois des Buttes in France. They were instructed to fight to the last man. An eyewitness recalls that he saw them surrounded by an innumerable and determined foe. The 2nd Devons mowed down large numbers of the enemy by the steadiness of their fire and their unshakable discipline, stated a report from the 23rd Infantry Brigade to the Headquarters, 8th Division of the British army.

This may have been the recollection of my grandfather, who said the enemy were coming through in such large numbers it seemed impossible to miss.

As it happened, 120 2nd Devons reported for duty at the end of the battle. One of them, Private 206044 Albert Edward Taylor, was later awarded the Military Medal for Gallantry in the Field. As a grandson, it made Hampton Grandad my boyhood hero.

25

Did King Arthur Discover America?

Well, he certainly would have been familiar with Armorica, the Roman name for Brittany in modern-day France.

According to reports in the Vatican Library, *Artorious* (Latin for Arthur) was the finest battle commander to have come out of Britannia. They had an auxiliary legion stationed in Armorica comprising British troops who had joined the Roman army. In return for twenty-five years of service, a soldier would be given a pension, an apartment, and an allotment. However, during this time in the army, they were not allowed to marry. Many formed informal relations with the comfort women based outside barracks. Maybe a soldier would marry his favourite lady on retirement. If he joined up at fifteen years old, he would be retired at forty. Perhaps this was why comfort ladies had an affinity with soldiery. The first- and second-oldest professions had a high regard for each other.

Come the withdrawal of the Roman army in the fifth century, it left places like Britain undefended, and auxiliary units were left to find new commissions. This could be why Arthur was called upon by the minor kingdoms remaining in Britain to form a viable defence against armed insurgents coming in from the east and the north east. His experience as a battle commander most likely would have him confirmed as the king of the Britons.

This is just another angle to the story of King Arthur, perhaps a practical one compared to the romantic historical stories we are more familiar with. Dissect romantics and we get Roman antics. The two could be of the same origin.

26

Nicholas de Meriet

Hardinge, the orphaned son of my earliest recorded ancestor, Alnoth, had two love children, according to records.

Nicholas the elder lived at the manor of Meriet in Somerset. About the year 1100 AD, surnames were given to the population to aid identification for the authorities. Had Nicholas been a thatcher by occupation, his surname would be have been Thatcher. Had he not been of age, his surname would have been Hardingson, after his father. If he was unusually short, his surname may have been Short.

He was a man of title, and his surname matched him to the manor of Meriet, a village in the county of Somerset. The modern spelling of the village is Merriott, whilst that of the surname is Merrett. My late maternal grandfather was Gilbert Alan Merrett, a surname associated with the west country, say the guidebooks, and I think they may be right. Somerset and Gloucestershire are the two counties where Merretts have been found mostly in historical records and on gravestones. There is a Merretts Farm in Standish and a Merretts Mill near Nailsworth, both in the county of Gloucestershire.

Merretts first appeared in Standish prior to the reign of Queen Elizabeth I, which started in 1558, and they have been there ever since. Content with farming-related activities set in a large parish, the family quietly went about their daily doings, unlike their Somerset ancestors, who were largely involved in senior soldiery and the great wars of English history until the lineage name died out due to lack of a male heir. Elizabeth Meriet was the last Meriet of Meriet, and she married a Beauchamp, whose name took over.

27

News Blackout

During the early hours of Easter Monday, Admiral Kirk and his crew safely transferred to our restored flagship HMS *Victory*. This historic occasion was subject to media silence given the gravity of the tactical deployment. He is now on the bridge with his Spock Navigator installed and taking our data transmissions.

For the record, the airborne transfer was made in our head of state version of the Merlin helicopter. Admiral Kirk sat back and admired the versatility of this medium lift multi-role combat aircraft as its three Rolls-Royce engines and five rotor blades powered it across a jet-black nighttime seascape.

His first message to our volunteer crews was broadcast at 0500 hrs GMT: "The Ocean, the current frontier. Our voyages of the Eurolanda fleet. Our indefinite mission: to explore the varied coastline, to seek out Europhiles and other undesirables, and deliver them safely to a former penal colony down under. To go where man has gone before. English-speaking people throughout the world expect our voluntary crews to do their duty."

It could probably go down in history as one of the finest 'finest hour' speeches ever delivered, changing the course of humanity.

28

Shipshape and Bristol Fashion

A volunteer crew prepare our restored starship HMS *Victory* ready for action at first light. They wear traditional seafaring clothes as the sails are hauled up the masts. Admiral Kirk studies his charts whilst his Spock Navigator prepares a route to the nearest coastal wind farm.

Turbine blades have been injuring and killing thousands of our migratory birds on their way to nesting in Great Britain, a practice outlawed on the mainland. Our Eurolanda fleet considers it has the moral right to destroy these pesky wind machines. The starship HMS *Victory* will deliver a broadside once in position on the Eurolanda coast from her anchorage in the Bristol Channel.

29

Black Panthers

For twenty years or more, there have been reports of black panthers living in the English countryside.

One summer I was driving an empty minibus on Over Causeway just west of Gloucester. Originally built by the Roman army as they pressed into South Wales from Glevum (Gloucester) to establish a new base at Caerleon next to the River Usk, this stronghold was still in use after the withdrawal of Roman forces from Britannicus beginning about 425 AD.

Eventually, it was where Arthur was crowned king of the Britons.

The former Roman road now joins the A40, an elevated section over Alney Island bypassing the city of Gloucester. It was along here that I glanced a black Labrador prowling alongside a hedgerow—but dogs don't prowl! A second glance revealed it was a big cat, or one of those black panthers that had been seen. It seemed perfectly logical that such a creature could support itself in the countryside. With plenty of lambs, sheep, rabbits, and pheasants about, it would probably have plenty to eat.

A second encounter told me these unconfirmed sightings were real. Driving another minibus from Parkend to Lydney in the Royal Forest of Dean, there on the grassy slope was a black panther in broad daylight prowling alongside a hedgerow.

Just a few years back, a farmer's wife out on a walk told me she had seen a black panther hunting deer. Apparently, that is their preferred choice of prey, and they ignore lambs and sheep and other game living in the wild.

The Black Panthers is also a name for my imaginary backing band, a troupe of ladies from Thailand. Now that is another tale!

30

Tales from the Great War

My dad had a way of getting Hampton Grandad to open up on his recollections of the First World War. For a long time after, he'd had nightmares and spoke little about it. Today it would be called posttraumatic stress disorder. He found his way of dealing with it was to remember the humorous parts over the sheer horror of it all. With me listening attentively as a young grandson, I remember his hair-raising accounts being told with a smile on his face.

He and his mate were on duty in the trenches when rations were handed out. Part of the pack was a type of hard biscuit. His friend had no teeth of his own so placed his on the floor of the trench. He then hit it with his rifle butt to break it up, but instead, it broke into powder and mixed well into the mud!

My grandad roared with laughter after he recalled that one.

Dad told me one where Grandad and his mate left the trenches at night and crawled through No Man's Land to the enemy positions. The task was to sabotage an observation balloon tethered by wire to the ground, the reward for which they were offered an extra weeks' leave. In their backpacks they carried wire cutters, which they used to cut the tethering wires. Just as they released the thing, Jerry (a German soldier) noticed it flying away and raised the alarm.

Grandad and his mate scarpered back towards British lines, but all hell let loose. They flung themselves into a shell crater and lay low until first light. It was only then they realised it had been full of sleeping enemy. They made it back to their own lines and lived to tell the tale. That story can be dated to the spring offensive of 1918 and what was to be the last enemy advance of the war.

Observation balloons carried troops to report on allied positions.

The goal was Paris, but it got no further than the River Aisne canals to the south west. It was here that the 2nd Devons were ordered to fight to the last to hold up the enemy whilst elements of the British and French armies withdrew across the Aisne to set up new defensive positions.

The heroic action of the 2nd Battalion, Devonshire Regiment didn't go unnoticed by the French. They were later awarded the Croix de Guerre, the only British regiment to receive the distinction throughout the duration of the Great War.

31

A Taylor's Tale

Maurice Edward Taylor, my dad, was eleven when the Second World War started. He recalled his family being sent gas masks and ration books long before the first action took place. There were air-raid siren practices, and windows of public buildings, reinforced with sandbags, were taped up as a precaution against bomb blasts.

The suburb where the family lived was by the River Thames, which was used by enemy bombers as a navigational aid on their way to London. Barrage balloons were set up to distract dive bombers and anti-aircraft gun positions set along the route. The authorities took the whole thing seriously, whereas the youngsters found it all amusing and fascinating. Even Hampton Grandad had built an Anderson shelter in the back garden, so all the family had protection during air raids. It could withstand anything except a direct hit.

Before long, enemy Heinkel and Messerschmitt bombers were going over in daylight formation, making for bombing raids over the docks in the East End of London. News was carried by BBC Radio in those days, and the family sometimes tuned into that and Lord Haw-Haw (William Joyce, who broadcast Nazi propaganda to the United Kingdom from Germany) for a laugh.

32

Black Panthers

Just how is a dynasty formed? Feline escapees from Southeast Asia have been seen over here for some time now.

Some come as cooks, and I've enjoyed all their native dishes. On the cusp of sweet or sour and quite spicy is how I like them. Frequenting their restaurant as a regular, little extras came my way: The odd glass of my favourite wine, rose, on the house, all served with a smile; complimentary mint chocolates with the coffee, all to the soothing sound of their background music, which I couldn't help but enjoy; gentle human I thought unlike us Brits who have learned how to complain from our consumer experts on TV and in the media.

Trying to get something off the bill seems to be a popular trait now—and not tipping. Demands for English food in an Indian restaurant seem to be the done thing. British beer in a Chinese another. Getting inebriated and vocal before dining out as part of a night's entertainment. Puking in a taxi driven by a Middle Eastern and bad language seem to be our pastimes. A famous international country built for and by the middle classes being trashed by consumerism and yob culture. Members of the opposite gender obsessed with having relationships and being shown commitment even though they overdo their wine. Useless, mindless sitting on a sofa watching never-ending soaps before pointless shopping trips where they overfill their wardrobes, cupboards, and wheelie bins.

The consumer lifestyle is sick. Conversation is out; confrontation between genders is in. Where is peace and quiet these days? Living independently is how I found it in large quantities and beneficial to my soul. A spiritual relationship is there for the taking and liberates my thinking, attitudes, and priorities.

The feline black panthers are very good at full-body massage too, I've found. Something not available on our NHS welfare curriculum but good for the health and well-being.

33

Skinny-Dipping

Three members of our voluntary crew soak up the sun off the starboard bow.

Admiral Kirk and his Spock have taken our restored HMS *Victory* into the warmer seas of the Mediterranean off Eurolanda. After leaving the Bristol Channel, his starship aimed a broadside at a coastal wind farm, causing damage.

Off Cadiz, the ship took up position in remembrance of the Battle of Trafalgar. Here, Nelson lost his life, but the English navy defeated a combined Spanish and French fleet without loss. The enemy lost all thirty-two ships. Some damaged hulks were towed into Gibraltar whilst others were lost in a storm. No wonder the phrase "Britannia rules the waves" came into existence and remains.

34

Full Sail Ahead

Far from the coast of Eurolanda, our tall ship makes waves. It has just offloaded a consignment of undesirables onto our modern container ship. Europhiles give themselves up under the weight of their own debt. Since Brexit, property prices have declined, so to the euro currency. Faced with a lifetime of negative equity and unaffordable debt, they would rather join our enterprise down under. Creditors are unlikely to come looking for them in the centre of the Outback!

Economic migrants who find no employment on the mainland can also join our enterprise rather than face the humiliation of going back to their country of origin empty handed.

A task of digging the world's largest man-made sea has appeal and a wonderful fulfilment factor to come on completion.

Eco-scientists, who have realised their global warming calculations were flawed, now begin trudging down to the coast and give themselves up to our Eurolanda fleet as they have no answer to their major miscalculations.

Psychists and climate protestors, illegal immigrants, and the gender neutered all have a place in the holds and an opportunity to make amends to their policy doubters.

35

Bois des Buttes 1918

Confusion surrounds much of the action that took place on Monday, 27 May 1918. The 2nd Battalion Devonshire Regiment were in positions north of the River Aisne on either side of a road leading through Bois des Buttes. The long-anticipated spring offensive by the German enemy began with a bombardment of more than four thousand artillery shells and a gas attack aimed at British and French forces. It was to be their last, leaving them about thirty miles short of Paris, their main objective.

The introduction of American armies had begun but had not yet been completed. Such was the strength of the enemy attack that allied troops were ordered back over the River Aisne and canals to take up new defensive positions. The 2nd Devons were to hold up this advance and were ordered to fight to the last bullet and last man. Those orders were prepared for all four companies of the battalion, but it was found in the aftermath that not all received those instructions. At least two of the messengers reporting to the company captains were killed in action en route. So the battalion as a whole was unprepared in part for the defensive action that was to take place.

The stand for the rest of the day by the 2nd Devons was of vital importance to the French army retreating to new positions on the British right. Their action did not go unnoticed.

The French nation awarded the entire 2nd Battalion Devonshire Regiment the Croix de Guerre for in the face of overwhelming odds they had faithfully held their ground and stemmed the enemy advance—the only British regiment to be awarded such throughout the duration of the Great War. After, they were permitted to wear a cockade of Croix de Guerre colours in their headdress on the anniversary of 27 May 1918 to commemorate the bravery shown by all ranks.

In 1920, a commemorative painting was commissioned for the officers' mess by war artist WB Wollen. It was hung in Exeter, where the Devonshire regiment was barracked in the United Kingdom and where it still remained around 1990 when shown to me by the museum curator.

Citations of the day for individual actions were sent to Brigade HQ, some of which were recommended for medal awards. It was not until 1919 that my grandfather Private 206044 Albert Edward Taylor received his Military Medal for Gallantry in the Field. It was whilst serving the regiment in the British army of the Rhine that had marched through to the west bank near Cologne two weeks after the armistice had been signed. By then, he said, he had forgotten exactly what he had done to attract the citation. Unfortunately, all were lost in the Second World War due to enemy bombing and flooding, so we shall never know!

36

Battlefield Clearance

The war of 1914–18 on the Western Front was fought mainly about a line running from the Belgian Coast through France to the Swiss border, a line that bent and bulged depending on military activity along its length. Hostilities had ceased at the eleventh hour on the eleventh day of the eleventh month in 1918.

The enemy army were given a fortnight to withdraw to the east bank of the River Rhine. They had to take their dead and wounded with them, as enemy burials were not permitted on French soil. So it can be imagined the train and extent of carts and wagons detailed for this purpose. Bodies were piled high where rural populations could see the transports trudge through their villages. Bodies removed from shallow graves were buried at the start of hostilities through to those corpses from the final year. The extent of decomposition was an affront to the senses of sight and smell. As it happened, the corpses were buried just inside enemy homeland, maybe as a protection for the folk of towns and cities who might have been even more horrified at the extent of their losses.

The French set aside areas for the burial of British and Commonwealth soldiers on land gifted to the mainly English-speaking people. The cemeteries neatly tended by the Imperial War Graves Commission can be seen all over Flanders, as it was sometimes known. Gravestones from England were each engraved at least with the soldier's name, rank and number, regiment and age. Those unidentified were placed in graves with the headstone inscribed A Soldier of the Great War Known unto God. One, known as The Tomb of the Unknown Soldier, was removed from the grave for ceremonial purposes and reburied in the Cenotaph, Whitehall, London. Each year since, a ceremony is carried out on Remembrance Sunday, where senior politicians and members of the Royal family lay a wreath of red poppies in memory of the fallen. It is the only time a monarch bows his head to a British subject. Thus, the Unknown Soldier is revered the highest status in the kingdom.

Back in France, the land had to be made good for farming again. It was said that every French cottage had an empty chair. Either a son or husband had not returned from the trenches. Such was the shortage of labour that forty thousand troops from the Chinese Labour Corps were lent for the purpose of battlefield clearance.

It took them a year.

37

International Leggings Brigade

One anonymous volunteer checks for intel as numbers begin swelling for a covert mission in Eurolanda tonight.

The Merlin helicopter can carry forty-five of our operatives to the drop zone and hover about before bringing them home again. They infiltrate the nightlife, mingling with the continental masses, starting with wine bars and then lager louts in the taverns. A multitude of shots may be required to get tongues wagging. Locals showing Europhile tendencies are reported to our Pixie Hat Regiment hidden nearby. The drunken swine are then airlifted in crates to our waiting container ship.

The groans of hangovers can be heard the following day on all decks, but their half world cruise will have already begun—albeit in container class cabins. The whole operation is reminiscent of how press gangs purportedly recruited for the Royal navy in thc good old days!

38

Tales from a Grandson

Dad recollected some of the First World War stories Grandad had told him.

One was about him being a sharpshooter. Stood on the fire step of a trench, he and his fellow 2nd Devons were engaging an enemy advance. Sometimes the standard issue Lee-Enfield rifle became so hot from firing that it seized up. A trained infantryman could fire one at the rate of fifteen rounds a minute, leading the enemy to sometimes believe they were actually firing machine guns. To carry on, they had to swap their rifle with that of a fallen or wounded colleague.

When the 2nd Battalion, Devonshire Regiment went into the advance on one occasion, Grandad probably heard the infamous order to fix bayonets. As they went over the top, they formed up into columns, each company having four to sixteen columns in total. As they made their way across No Man's Land, Grandad saw men falling to his left and to his right, their places simply taken by another from the rear. He also saw the enemy fleeing from their lines in droves. Their own officers shot at any that turned to run. An officer was one of the first targeted by the advancing troops, thus sparing enemy lives and giving them the chance to give themselves up.

39

Hometown

Regency Cheltenham Spa has its own parish church as the oldest known building. It was built in the thirteenth century, when the town was still a hamlet. In the same century it was granted a weekly market, and that's when it gained town status.

Before then it was in the shadow of nearby Prestbury. Both were on a route from Gloucester: The Cathedral City to Winchcombe Abbey and beyond Hailes Abbey.

It was a travelling doctor from London who noticed a spring between that route and the River Chelt. He discovered it had medicinal qualities, which led to national fame and its status as a spa town.

It's described nowadays as the finest inland resort in the country with everything, bar the seaside! Gustav Holst, the composer of the Planet Suite, lives here. Poet laureate Alfred Lord Tennyson lived here opposite the railway terminus when it first opened. The Duke of Wellington retired here after defeating Napoleon at Waterloo and a spell as being prime minister living in our London Road. King George even reigned from here for six weeks whilst staying with his queen and family in Bayshill close to the spa that then became known as Royal Well.

Some US forces camped in our Pittville Park during 1944 whilst preparations were made for the D-Day landings. Brian Jones, founder of the Rolling Stones, grew up in the neighbouring parish of Hatherley.

That's all for now, folks!

40

Celtic Briton

Earliest humans set foot in Britain when it was still connected to the Eurolanda mainland. The hunter-gatherer probably followed deer herds as they made their way north during the summer months and then south again for the winter. A practice similar to that is followed in some parts of Lapland and Canada today. Weaponry was likely to have been the spear and later the bow and arrow.

Earliest humans, therefore, were not settlers but had a nomadic lifestyle.

The first settlers are described as Celtic. They had the ability to build themselves shelters and early farmsteads. Julius Caesar noted that Britannia was well populated and that many farmsteads had grey geese as livestock. That was a source of eggs and feathers supplemented by hunting trips for deer, giving them hides and antlers as well as meat.

It seems that the early Briton began populating the now island from the west to the east. Study of DNA suggests a kind of Scando-Iberian origin close to the Atlantic area spreading eastwards. That suggests they had come here by sea and so could add fish to their diet. Many early settlements were built alongside rivers, which gave water for fishing, washing, and somewhere to tie the boat.

The more advanced Mediterranean civilizations sent their merchant trading vessels. Tin was available from mines in Cornwall on the southwestern tip of the island. Without it, the Bronze Age could not have begun. The alloy being a mix of tin and bronze was found elsewhere.

Early dynasties controlled mining and negotiated trade deals with the merchant fleets. The name of the metal survives in the place named Tintagel, built close to the sea and eventually protected by a castle. The patriarch almost certainly took the title king when the early kingdom of heaven spread from Jerusalem. His enlarged territory becoming known as Cornwall—then a kingdom, now a county in the United Kingdom. The seat for the king of Cornwall was Tintagel, who probably gained his wealth from trading tin.

The castle later gave birth to their most famous son, Arthur, king of the Britons. But that is another story!

41

International Leggings Brigade

One of our anonymous volunteers checks for intel while waiting for a beverage. A party of them where brought back from Eurolanda by the Merlin helicopter in the early hours of this morning.

Sounding out corrupt EU climate liars who are destined for our prestige project in the centre of a former penal colony down under was likely their target. Nobody knows!

They live in a provincial town whose authorities fancy it as becoming the cyber capital of the United Kingdom. More than four thousand new homes are being built west of the town centre around a cyber park for that purpose and could well be a future barracks for our brigade!

42

Yardarm

After a good catch, the holds on our voluntary tall ship were crammed with undesirables from the mainland of Eurolanda. Excess numbers were given a beam to cling to and a rope to stand on.

Let's hope their introduction to traditional shipping methods doesn't allow them to drop off. For some, it would be straight into the drink below—for others, a drop onto the deck. Ouch!

43

Patron Saint

On 23 April each year in the United Kingdom is St George's Day, the patron saint of England. His story originates from the Middle East, where a damsel was left tied to a tree in order to pacify a dragon that would otherwise attack her village.

Just as the dragon was about to turn her into his next meal, along came George, a knight in shining armour, and slew the dragon. He freed the maiden and swept her off her feet onto his horse and rode off into the sunset. They lived happily ever after, or something like that.

Somehow, that got him the patronage of England and elsewhere.

Andrew was made the patron saint of Scotland and Patrick that of Ireland.

Their three flags combined make for the combined flag of Great Britain as shown in the top left-hand quarter of the Brexiteer standard.

44

King of the Britons

Arthur had a mentor even before he was conceived. Merlin the Wizard, by his trickery, arranged for King Uther Pendragon to sleep with the Queen of Cornwall at Tintagel Castle on the same day as she was widowed. They shortly married. Arthur was therefore born in wedlock but conceived before the marriage. As agreed, Merlin took Arthur away to be brought up as his own. He found a couple of royal status to give the young lad parentage, although not his own. Merlin's tutorage included military training at what would now be officer level. It's possible that this was in a Roman army school, who put the trained Arthur in charge of an auxiliary legion based in Armorica, now Brittany in France. Latin records later state that he was the finest battle commander to have come out of Britannia.

When Roman forces began withdrawing from across Europe towards Rome, auxiliary legions were abandoned. Armed militia from beyond the rivers Rhine and Danube invaded and pressed the Roman armies further into withdrawal. Britain was left abandoned, but a senior Roman official by thc name of Vortigern remained to do the best he could against armed invaders coming into the east and northeast of the island. To this end he hired a former auxiliary legion from Saxony who were based by him on the Isle of Sheppey in the River Thames Estuary. He fell in love with their princess and eventually made her his queen. However, he ran short of money, so the Saxon army mutinied and took up self-sufficiency and farming.

It was the opportunity for the remaining minor kingdoms of western Britain to unite and take over the whole island. The man for the job was Arthur, with both his experience as a battle commander and royal lineage and his right-hand man, Merlin the Wizard, who revealed Arthur's suitability to the assembled minor kingdoms. After some dissent, Arthur wrestled power from the dissenters and was made king of the Britons. This was symbolised by his taking the sword from the stone outside St Paul's Abbey in London. His coronation was at Caerleon, in what is now Wales. Further invaders came in from the East Coast and the north, including Jutes, Picts, Angles, and others.

Somehow, the Anglo and Saxon armies united to give Arthur his strongest opposition. He and his armies fought the Anglo-Saxons in a series of twelve battles. It was the final battle at Baddon Hill just outside Plymouth where the two opposing armies met. The Britons assembled under a banner featuring a red dragon as its emblem. The Anglo-Saxon army under a white dragon were crushed by the Britons, and King Arthur achieved the goal of an island ruled by the British.

He assembled his true faithful leaders at Winchester and created the Knights of the Round Table as his deputies in running the kingdom. The motto of the new realm was Truth and Justice.

45

Black Panthers

Two of our volunteer night operators stop for a snack and a beverage.

Airlifted from Eurolanda in the early hours this morning, the Merlin helicopter again obligingly dropped them off somewhere close to home.

46

The Beetles

At the end of World War II, the former enemy needed assistance getting industry going again. Factories that were converted to making weaponry and ammunitions needed new investment and senior management to get them going again in the peacetime economy. Finance came from the United States in the form of McCarthy Loans and directorship from the United Kingdom.

One such was John Harvey-Jones, a former Army officer who helped get the 'Folks Wagon' into production (or Volkswagen, as it is more commonly known). This eased some of the employment problems felt there after the war, and soon they were knocking them out twenty to the dozen. They hit on a bit of a winner, but not without its problems. The decision to use an air-cooled engine ran into trouble when the vehicle was in a queue of traffic and heated up very quickly, particularly in the summer. Mounting it at the rear and not using adequate soundproofing made conversation between passengers that more difficult. Still, it developed into something of a cult car and could often be seen on our roads amongst the Citroens and Fiats of similar overseas production.

John Harvey-Jones came back to Britain and went into the chemicals industry. He put together a consortium of companies, becoming known as ICI, or Imperial Chemical Industries, which for many years was something of a bellwether on the UK stock market.

He retired as Sir John Harvey-Jones and soon became well known for a TV series called *Troubleshooter.* He lent his industrial expertise to small- and medium-sized businesses in an attempt to get them remotivated and focused.

One intending passenger saw me reading *Troubleshooter* at a timing point one afternoon. He remarked that Sir John Harvey-Jones was the best prime minister we never had!

47

Star Date 182023.4

Admiral Kirk has already boosted morale amongst our voluntary crews of the Eurolanda fleet. Their purpose: To seek out the scoundrels on the mainland, converting them to the labour force for our superb project down under.

The purpose and value of a man-made inland sea in the middle of the desert Outback is plain to any visionary worth his or her salt. Desalination plants on the coast of the continent would ensure that freshwater is fed to the centre via a navigable canal. Introduced fish stocks will mean early settlers have foodstuff, and irrigation ditches will ensure vegetable supply and likely also orchard trees when grown. Real estate developers can produce the finest inland resort in the world.

The hard labour of the current undesirables of the EU will have been all worth it and of great benefit to future generations of all nationalities. Miscreants making up the labour force having their internationally agreed minimum wages accumulated for their dotage could sit back and enjoy the fruits of their labours.

Even the Spock Navigator says it's all logical!

48

British and Continental

EU driving hours regulations wiped the smile off the jovial coach driver's face.

The spy in the cab tachograph was introduced at the same time as HGV lorry drivers came under the legislation.

Analogue discs had to be kept for six months and between twenty-eight to forty-two days in the cab with the driver. Fines were imposed for anyone infringing this law.

Four and a half hours continuous driving was set as a maximum. On-the-spot fines in the EU were imposed for any infringements.

Drivers could still come under UK domestic driving hours regulations, which allowed five and a half hours continuous driving as a maximum when driving in the United Kingdom on scheduled timetabled services. Rest periods had to be a minimum of forty-five minutes or split fifteen minutes and then thirty minutes in any four and a half hours of driving under EU regulations, but only thirty minutes under UK rules. The length of the driving day was limited to nine hours in a fifteen-hour duty, followed by a minimum nine hours' rest before driving again under EU rules. However, twice in a week, a driver could drive for up to ten hours in a day under EU rules. Confused yet?

Considerable anxiety occurred every day as a driver. If the traffic slowed on the motorway, it could add hours to a journey. The tachograph recorded the driving time, not the distance driven. Drivers had to find a suitable rest area and take their statutory rest break or risk breaching driving hours regulations and lose their job. Fury was experienced from passengers who were trying to get to an airport on time or change coaches at a terminal for longer journeys. Was this the intention of the EU policymakers, to make coach travel worse? Was the coach industry even consulted before these regulations were brought in? No they ruddy weren't!

49

Motorway Madness

The standard motorway in the United Kingdom has three lanes: A nearside lane, a middle lane for overtaking, and an outside lane for overtaking. HGV and PCV (lorries and coaches) were banned from using the outside lane. The lorry industry introduced speed limiters on their vehicles, limiting their speed to fifty-six miles an hour. The coach industry did the same at sixty-two mph, although the legal limit was seventy!

The result was that a coach could use the middle lane to overtake say a line of HGVs before moving back to the nearside, the passing speed being only six mph more than the HGVs. It could take ages to pass a line of lorries. Cars and light vans in the middle lane, in order to maintain their seventy mph, had to use the outside lane to overtake. If this lane was already congested, you can imagine the line of cars and vans stuck behind the coach!

Worse still, an empty HGV could pull into the middle lane doing fifty-six mph in order to overtake a line of laden lorries struggling to maintain their limited top speed.

The result was that a coach doing sixty-two mph in the middle lane could suddenly find itself behind an HGV doing only fifty-six. The coach could not overtake the lorry as it is banned from the outside lane. That made scheduled journey time even longer and more frustrating, as this could occur many times on a motorway journey. No wonder the coach industry has been permanently short of drivers for decades. Inhumane driving hours regulations and congested motorways are partially to blame. The pay is pretty reasonable if you get a tip from fifty different passengers for a day trip. My-Skool-Bus drivers don't get gratuities off the kids, just litter left on the floor!

50

Russian Rush Hour

It was a Friday afternoon, probably late autumn, and I was sent up to London Heathrow Airport to meet and greet a Russian couple and their son arriving from Moscow. Unusual in that I'd never met a Russian before during my time as a professional driver or elsewhere.

The task was to take them to a local independent boarding school where their boy was due to continue his education, wait, and then take his mum and dad to a hotel where they were staying for the weekend.

It was busy at the airport as the multi-storey car park was near full. I found a space near the top floor and then went by foot into the terminal. That was busy too, and the flight I was due to meet was showing a delay of about thirty minutes.

Nothing unusual in that as I did a quick mental calculation and realised we would be leaving right in the middle of the notorious peak traffic time as London discharged its workforce and visitors to the provinces and suburbs for the evening.

Anyway, the trio came through with the crowds at Arrivals and spotted me waiting with their name on a board. We acknowledged each other in the din and realised our language barrier meant we more understood each other with a few nods and hand gestures than with verbal.

They followed me back to the car, the luggage went into the boot, and the largish parents took up much of the backseats. The young scholar took the passenger seat in the front. I drove towards the exit ramps and found we were stuck in a queue almost straight away. We were several levels up from the ground exit and made notoriously slow progress heading down the ramps. About half an hour had passed before we emerged from the car park into a traffic jam. From the terminal to the motorway, we lost another half hour in the queues.

Eventually, I broke the silence and apologised for the slow progress.

The father replied in English with a Russian accent, "Don't worry, it's worse than this in Russia."

We laughed and had broken the ice between us. From then on it was a joy and a privilege to drive them the near one hundred miles in the darkness and stop-start traffic.

51

Star Date 192023.4

We're downloading an upgrade of our intel systems to all vessels of the Eurolanda fleet. Admiral Kirk will be aided by a Spockometer, replacing the Spock Navigator, giving him more bites on the starboard bows.

Indications are that the opening of the Brexiteer campaign has reached a suitable size for downloading into paperback, hardback, and audiobook retrieval systems available for purchase by standard retail methods.

As the operation is now going into covert mode, further communications will be terminated until sometime soon.

We thank you for following the short communiques so far aimed entirely at English-speaking people like us.

Roger and out!

52

On-the-Spot Fine

A coach company I worked for in North Somerset has a regular day trip to France and Belgium, where passengers can shop at a Hypermarket just outside Calais and then buy duty-free tobacco products, wines, spirits, and perfumes from warehouses just over the Belgium border.

It was a popular trip, where the fare was more than offset by the price savings available on the continent. We collected punters from Taunton, Bridgewater, Weston Super Mare, and Bristol before setting off for Ashford in Kent to take the Eurotunnel into France.

It was a two-driver job to comply with EU driving hours regulations. The first driver went as far as Ashford, and then a changeover to the second driver for the French and Belgium return leg of the trip. The first driver again made the journey back to the west country from the Eurotunnel.

Predicting the duration of the journey was fine on paper, but traffic delays and customs officers work to rules on the day could lead to drivers being out of hours before finishing the job.

To combat that, our traffic office could monitor the progress of the coach using GPS, and if need be, arrange for a third driver to take over at a motorway service area to complete the journey. Otherwise, the two original drivers would have to complete a minimum nine-hour rest period before continuing. Not very popular with their wives and girlfriends—or punters for that matter. Or the drivers themselves!

Inconsistent working hours was another reason the whole UK industry was short of coach drivers overall. Matters outside their control, excessive driving hours regulations, and on-the-spot fines combined to make the job excessively antisocial in what was otherwise a classic occupation.

By comparison, a self-employed taxi driver could work whatever hours he or she liked without any statutory limitations. This was an industry where at times there were too many drivers and not enough paying passengers. Some drivers took up courier work to take up the slack, and others worked part time for local coach companies on school contracts (for example) to work closer to home. I know I did!

Printed in thc United States
by Baker & Taylor Publisher Services